Martina
the Beautiful Cockroach

Published by
PEACHTREE PUBLISHERS
1700 Chattahoochee Avenue
Atlanta, Georgia 30318-2112
www.peachtree-online.com

Text © 2007 by Carmen Agra Deedy
Illustrations © 2007 by Michael Austin

Illustrations created in acrylic on Strathmore Series 500 illustration board. Titles created with Nick Curtis's Fontleroy Brown; text typeset in International Typeface Corporation's Belwe Light.

Printed in Singapore
10 9 8 7 6 5 4 3

Library of Congress Cataloging-in-Publication Data

Deedy, Carmen Agra.
  Martina the beautiful cockroach : a Cuban folktale / retold by Carmen Agra Deedy ; illustrated by Michael Austin. — 1st ed.
    p. cm.
  Summary: In this humorous retelling of a Cuban folktale, a cock-roach interviews her suitors in order to decide whom to marry.
  ISBN 13: 978-1-56145-399-3 ISBN 10: 1-56145-399-4
  [1. Cockroaches—Folklore. 2. Folklore—Cuba.] I. Austin, Michael, 1965- ill. II. Title.
  PZ8.1.D3782Mar 2007
  398.2—dc22
  [E]
                              2007003108

In memory of Abuela Graciela and Abuela Ofelia.

Thanks to my family, of course:
Papi and Mami; Katie, Erin, and Lauren;
Tersi, Ben, and Jordan.
And a special note of thanks to the children of
Holy Innocents' School and Davis Academy.

—*C. A. D.*

For Dad and Elisa

—*M. A.*

Martina
the Beautiful Cockroach

A CUBAN FOLKTALE

RETOLD BY
CARMEN AGRA DEEDY

ILLUSTRATED BY
MICHAEL AUSTIN

Ω
PEACHTREE
ATLANTA

Martina Josefina Catalina Cucaracha was a beautiful cockroach.

She lived in a cozy street lamp in Old Havana with her big, lovable family.

Now that Martina was 21 days old, she was ready to give her leg in marriage. The Cucaracha household was crawling with excitement! Every *señora* in the family had something to offer.

Tía Cuca gave her *una peineta*, a seashell comb.

Mamá gave her *una mantilla*, a lace shawl.

But *Abuela,* her Cuban grandmother, gave her *un consejo increíble*, some shocking advice.

"You want me to do WHAT?" Martina was aghast.

"You are a beautiful cockroach," said *Abuela*. "Finding husbands to choose from will be easy—picking the right one could be tricky."

"B-b-but," stammered Martina, "how will spilling COFFEE on a suitor's shoes help me find a good husband?"

Her grandmother smiled. "It will make him angry! Then you'll know how he will speak to you when he loses his temper. Trust me, Martina. The Coffee Test never fails."

Martina wasn't so sure.

Meanwhile, *Papá* sent *el perico,* the parrot,
to spread the word.

Soon all Havana—from the busy sidewalks of
El Prado to El Morro castle—was abuzz with the news.

Martina the beautiful cockroach was ready
to choose a husband.

As was the custom, Martina would greet
her suitors from the balcony, under her family's
many watchful eyes.
Daintily, she sat down
and crossed her legs,
and crossed her legs,
and crossed her legs.

She didn't have long to wait.

Don Gallo, the rooster, strutted up first. Martina tried not to stare at his splendid shoes.

Keeping one eye on his reflection, Don Gallo greeted her with a sweeping bow. "*¡Caramba!* You really are a beautiful cockroach. I will look even more fabulous with you on my wing!"

With that, he leaned forward and crooned,

> "Martina
>> Josefina
>>> Catalina
>>>> Cucaracha,
>>> Beautiful *muchacha*,
>> Won't you be my wife?"

Martina hesitated only for an instant. "Coffee, *señor*?"

Right on cue, *Abuela* appeared.

With a quick glance at her grandmother, Martina nervously splattered coffee onto the rooster's spotless shoes.

"Oh my!" she said with mock dismay. "I'm all feelers today!"

"*¡Ki-ki-ri-kiiii!*" The rooster was furious. "Clumsy cockroach! I will teach you better manners when you are my wife."

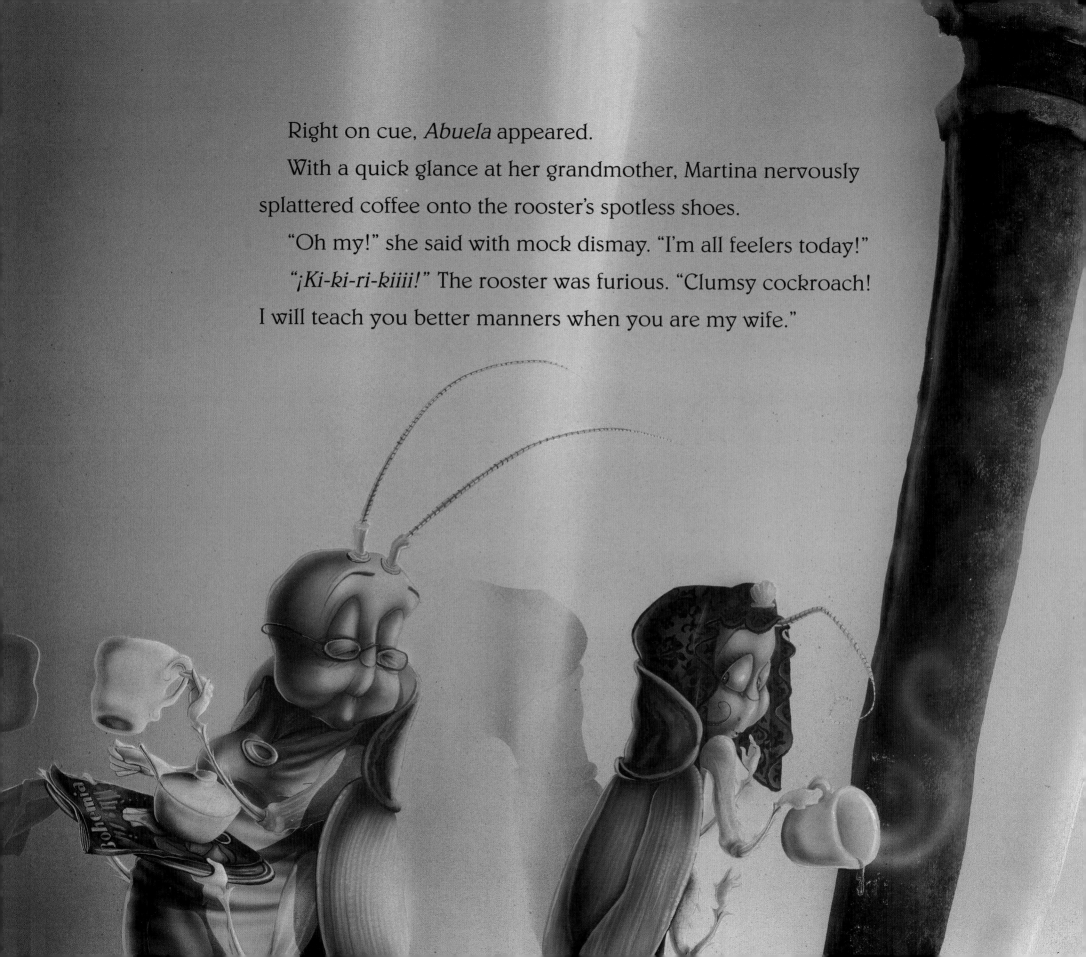

Martina was stunned.
The Coffee Test had worked!
"A most humble offer, *señor*,"
she said cooly, "but I cannot accept.
You are much too cocky for me."

Don Cerdo, the pig, hoofed up next. His smell curled the little hairs on Martina's legs.

"What an unimaginable scent," Martina wheezed. "Is it some new pig cologne?"

"Oh no, *señorita*. It's the sweet aroma of my pig sty. Rotten eggs! Turnip peels! Stinky cheese!" Don Cerdo licked his chops and sang,

"Martina
Josefina
Catalina
Cucaracha,
Beautiful *muchacha*,
Won't you be my wife?"

Martina had already left in search of coffee.

She wasted no time with the pig.

"*¡Gronc! ¡Gronc!*" squealed Don Cerdo
as he dabbed at the coffee on his shoes.
"What a tragedy for my poor loafers!"

He really is quite a ham,
thought Martina.

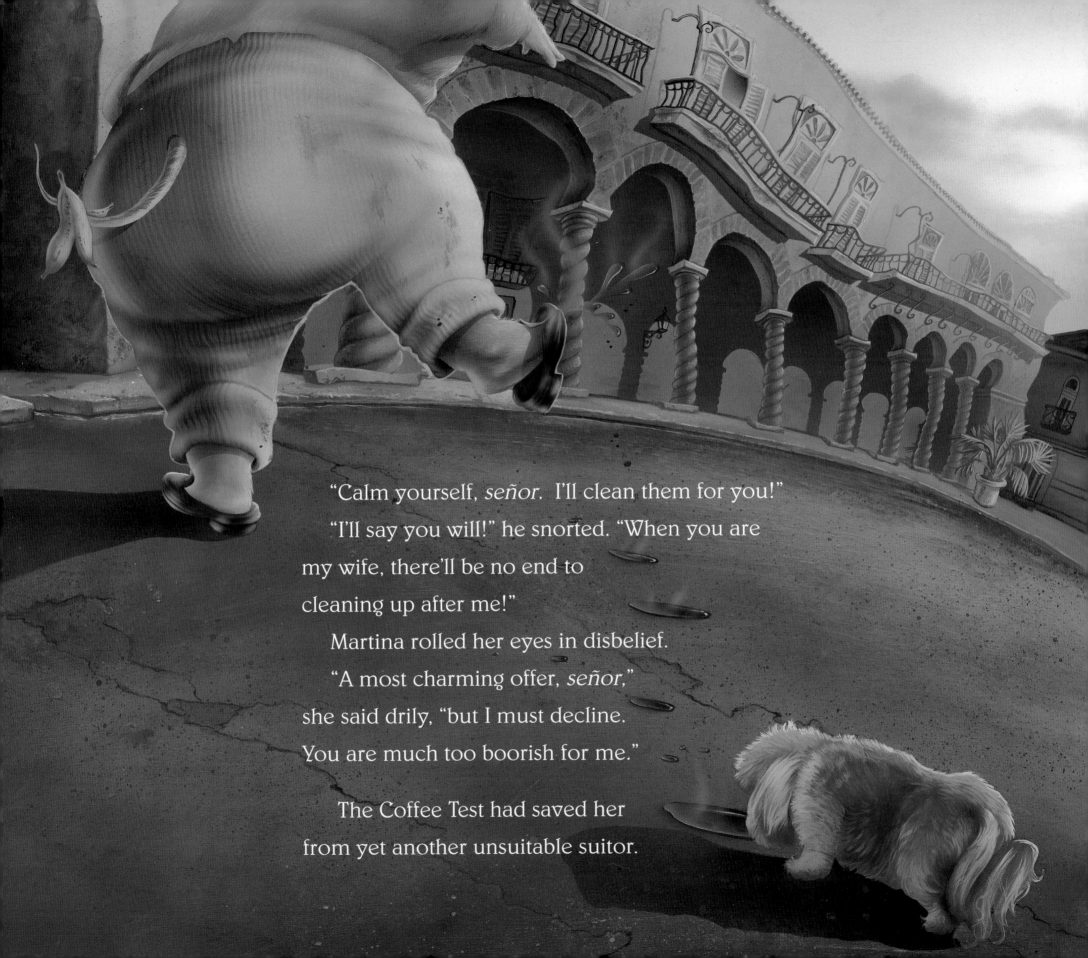

"Calm yourself, *señor.* I'll clean them for you!"

"I'll say you will!" he snorted. "When you are
my wife, there'll be no end to
cleaning up after me!"

Martina rolled her eyes in disbelief.

"A most charming offer, *señor,*"
she said drily, "but I must decline.
You are much too boorish for me."

The Coffee Test had saved her
from yet another unsuitable suitor.

The pig was scarcely out of sight when Don Lagarto, the lizard, crept over the railing. His oily fingers brushed the little cockroach's lovely *mantilla*.

"You shouldn't sneak up on a lady like that!"

"I don't sneak. I creep," he said, circling Martina.

For some reason this fellow really bugged her. "I've had enough of creeps for one day," said Martina. *"Adiós."*

"But I need you! Wait!" The lizard fell on one scaly knee and warbled,

> "Martina
>> Josefina
>>> Catalina
>>>> Cucaracha,
>>> Beautiful *muchacha*,
>> Won't you be my wife?"

Martina sighed. "Let me see if there's any coffee left."

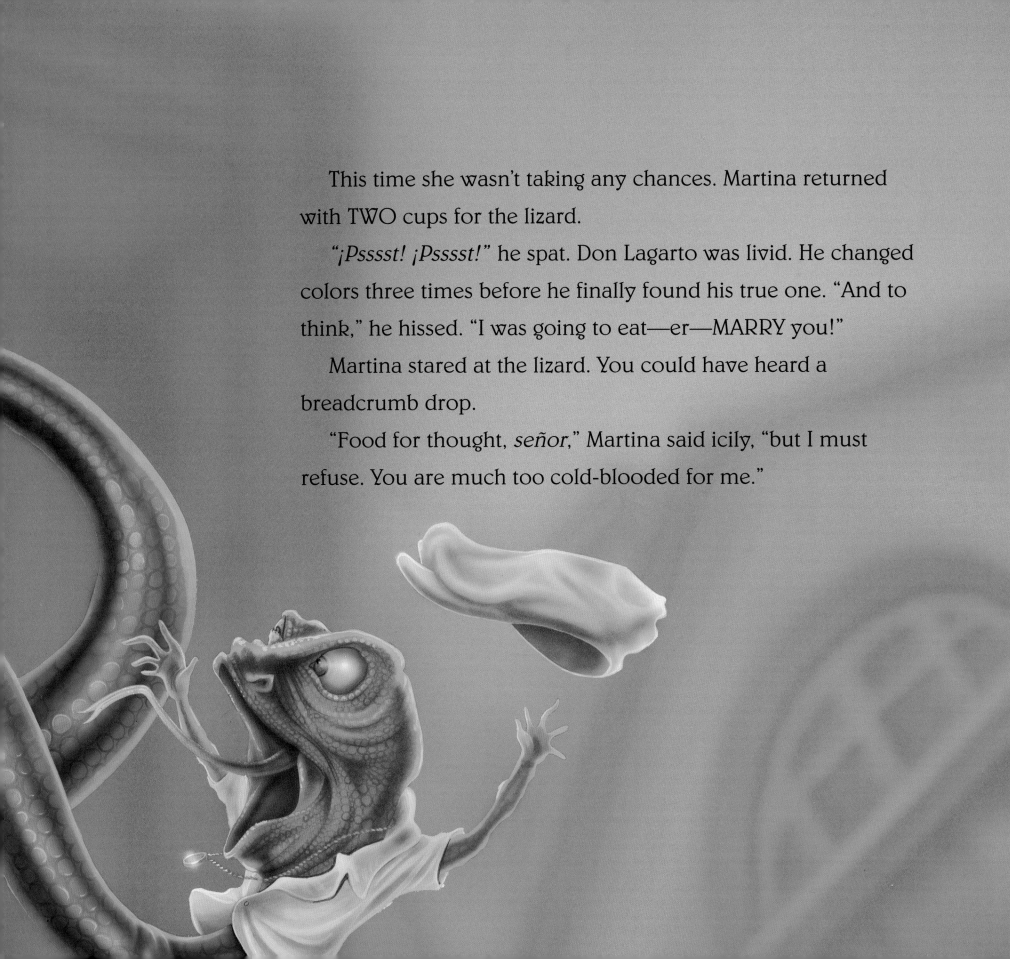

This time she wasn't taking any chances. Martina returned with TWO cups for the lizard.

"*¡Psssst! ¡Psssst!*" he spat. Don Lagarto was livid. He changed colors three times before he finally found his true one. "And to think," he hissed. "I was going to eat—er—MARRY you!"

Martina stared at the lizard. You could have heard a breadcrumb drop.

"Food for thought, *señor*," Martina said icily, "but I must refuse. You are much too cold-blooded for me."

When her grandmother returned to collect the day's coffee cups, Martina was still fuming.

"I'm going inside, *Abuela*."

"So soon?"

"*¡Si!* I'm afraid of whom I might meet next!"

Abuela drew Martina to the railing and pointed to the garden below. "What about him?"

Martina looked down at the tiny brown mouse, and her cockroach heart began to beat faster.

> *Ti-ki-tin, ti-ki-tan.*

"Oh, *Abuela*, he's adorable. Where has he been?"

"Right here all along."

"What do I do?"

"Go talk to him...and just be yourself."

Martina handed *Abuela* her *peineta* and *mantilla*, then scurried down to the garden. The mouse was waiting.

    Ti-ki-tin, ti-ki-tan.

"*Hola*, hello." His voice was like warm honey. "My name is Pérez."

"*Hola*," she whispered shyly, "I'm Martina—"

"—the beautiful cockroach," he finished for her.

"You think I'm beautiful?"

The little mouse turned pink under his fur. "Well, my eyes are rather weak, but I have excellent EARS. I know you are strong and good, Martina Josefina Catalina Cucaracha." Then he squinted sweetly. "*Who cares if you are beautiful?*"

    TI-KI-TIN, TI-KI-TAN.

"Martina-a-a-a-a! Don't forget the coffee!" It was *Abuela*.

No, thought Martina. No coffee for Pérez!

"Martina Josefina Catalina Cucaracha!"

"*Sí, Abuela.*" Martina knew better than to argue with her Cuban grandmother.

With a heavy heart, she reached for the cup.

But Pérez got there first.
Quick as a mouse, he splashed
café cubano onto Martina's shoes.

Now the coffee was on the other foot.

Martina was too delighted to
be angry. At last, she'd found her
perfect match. But she had
to ask, "How did you know
about the Coffee Test?"

Pérez grinned. "Well, *mi amor*,
my love…

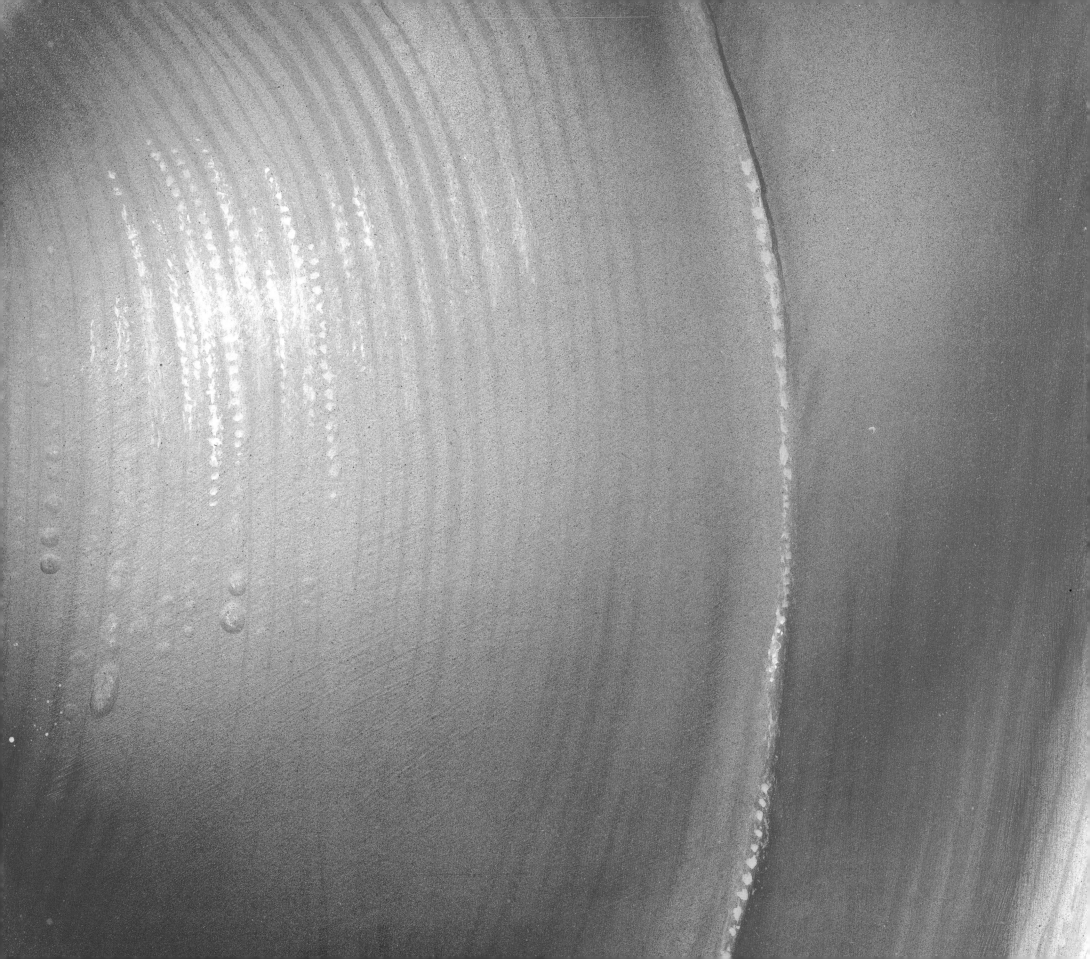